This book belongs to

_____

The
Ugly Duckling

BY

Hans Christian Andersen

Retold by Jennifer Greenway

ILLUSTRATED BY

Robyn Officer

TED SMART

A TED SMART Publication 1995

First published in the USA in 1992 by Andrews and McMeel

ISBN 0 7529 0112 5

Design: Susan Hood and Mike Hortens
Art Direction: Armand Eisen, Mike Hortens and Julie Phillips
Art Production: Lynn Wine
Production: Julie Miller and Lisa Shadid

The Ugly Duckling

One lovely summer day, on the bank of a quiet pond beside an old farmhouse, a duck sat on her nest waiting for her eggs to hatch.

First a crack appeared on one egg, then on another, and another. Little ducklings began to poke their heads out of the shells.

7

The mother duck was delighted until she noticed that one egg still had not hatched. This egg was larger than the others and a dull gray color.

The mother duck sighed. She was about to sit on the nest awhile longer when one of the older ducks in the pond came by. She asked the mother duck about her ducklings and then said, "I wouldn't bother trying to hatch that egg if I were you. It looks like a turkey egg to me. I hatched one once by

mistake, and it caused me no end of trouble. Leave that egg alone and come teach your ducklings to swim!"

But the mother duck replied that she had been sitting on her nest so long already, a little more time wouldn't matter. And she settled onto her nest and waited patiently.

Presently, the mother duck heard a sharp crack, and out popped the last duckling. But what a strange duckling he was! He was twice as big as the others, and had gray feathers instead of yellow.

Even his mother had to admit he was rather ugly. "Oh, dear," she thought. "Perhaps it was a turkey egg after all!"

The next morning, she led her ducklings to the pond to teach them how to swim. The ugly duckling jumped right in the water and swam with no trouble.

"Well, he can't be a turkey, if he can swim as well as that," his mother said to herself. "Besides, if you look at him properly, he isn't so ugly!"

Feeling very proud, the mother duck called her ducklings out of the water. Then she led them to the barnyard to introduce them to the other ducks.

"Be sure to behave yourselves," she told them as they walked through the grass. "And don't forget to say 'quack' and bow politely to everyone."

In the barnyard, the ducklings did as they were told. They bowed politely to everyone and said "quack." The other ducks looked them over carefully. "Your ducklings are all very well behaved," one of the old ducks said at last. "And they are all very pretty—except for that big gray one. He is the ugliest duckling I've ever seen!"

All the other ducks in the barnyard agreed, and even the ugly duckling's brothers and sisters began to make fun of him.

"He is ugly," replied his mother, "but he is clever and polite and means no harm."

"Very well," sniffed the other ducks. "He can stay, so long as he stays out of sight."

The other ducklings quickly made themselves at home. But from that moment on, everyone in the barnyard was mean to the ugly duckling. His brothers and sisters kicked him and bit him. The older ducks chased him. The hens and roosters pecked him. One day, even his mother admitted that she wished he had never been born.

When he heard that, the ugly duckling decided to run away, and he flew over the hedge and into the fields. He soon came to the marsh where the wild ducks lived, and there he fell asleep.

When he awoke, the wild ducks were standing around him, staring curiously.

"What are you?" they said. "We have never seen a duck like you before."

"I don't know myself," replied the ugly duckling shyly.

"It is only that you are so very ugly!" said the wild ducks. "But you seem nice enough, so you may stay with us if you like."

The grateful ugly duckling flew with the wild ducks over the marsh. Suddenly there were loud popping sounds. Hunters in the marsh below were firing their guns at the wild ducks! The poor ducks all dropped into the water—dead.

The ugly duckling was terrified and hid among the reeds. A hunting dog ran past him, baring his fangs. But the dog did not stop.

"Ah," the ugly duckling thought sadly. "I am so ugly that even a dog won't bite me." He sat very still until the hunters left. Then he flew alone toward the forest.

The ugly duckling flew until he was so tired that he could hardly flap his wings. It was evening by then, and a storm was gathering. Soon rain began to fall. Cold and hungry, the ugly duckling was happy to see the light of a cottage ahead. He flew toward it, and, finding the door open, he went inside.

The cottage belonged to an old woman who lived there with her big tomcat and her prize red hen. When they saw the ugly duckling, the hen began to cluck and the cat began to hiss.

"What is it?" cried the old woman, who was very nearsighted. When she caught sight of the ugly duckling she thought he was a nice fat duck who had run away from a nearby farm. "Oh, good!" she said. "Now I shall have duck's eggs to eat." She fed the ugly duckling some bread and water and told him he could stay if he liked.

This did not please the cat or the hen at all, for they liked to think that they were master and mistress of the household. After the old woman had gone to bed, they turned on the ugly duckling.

"Can you lay eggs?" clucked the hen.

"No," replied the ugly duckling.

"Can you arch your back and purr?" hissed the cat.

"No," replied the ugly duckling.

"Then what good are you?" said the cat.

"Can't you do anything at all?" said the hen.

"I can swim," replied the ugly duckling. Then he told them how lovely the water felt and what fun it was to dive to the bottom.

"Fun!" cried the hen. "Why, it sounds horrible!"

"Dreadful!" agreed the cat. "You had better learn to purr or lay eggs, or you won't be here much longer."

Then the cat scratched the ugly duckling, and the hen pecked him, until the poor creature decided he had better leave.

So the ugly duckling flew to a quiet pond in the middle of the forest. There, he could swim and dive all day long. But he was careful to hide from all the other creatures, because he had grown ashamed of his ugliness.

Autumn came. Leaves fell from the trees and the wind grew sharp. The days were growing shorter, and the nights were getting colder. It would soon be winter. It was becoming harder to find food, and the ugly duckling was hungry and lonely.

One cool evening, he was resting at the edge of the pond and gazing at the sunset, when he saw a great flock of birds flying overhead.

The birds were the most beautiful the ugly duckling had ever seen. They were white as snow, with wide, strong wings and long, graceful necks. The ugly duckling did not know it, but these were swans flying south for the winter. Suddenly, they spread their wings and all together uttered a cry unlike anything the ugly duckling had ever heard. Then they flew on, their feathers gleaming in the last rays of the sun.

The ugly duckling stared after them. Then without realizing it, he arched his neck and called back to them—a cry so strange it frightened him. No living creature had ever made him feel that way before. How he wished he could be as lovely as those proud, white birds were! "But what would such royal birds say if they were to see me?" he thought sadly.

Soon cruel winter came. The ugly duckling had to swim in a circle all day to keep the pond from freezing over. Each day, the circle in which he could swim grew smaller and smaller. One day, it was so cold that, despite the ugly duckling's efforts, the pond completely froze. The poor ugly duckling could not swim another stroke, and he fell exhausted on the ice.

The next morning, a peasant passing by
saw the ugly duckling lying on the ice.
Feeling sorry for him, the peasant picked up
the poor little bird and carried him home.

His wife put the ugly duckling next to
the fire. Soon he warmed up and began
to spread his wings. When the peasant's
children saw this, they came running toward
him, for they wanted to play with the duckling.

The ugly duckling was so frightened that he beat his wings, knocking over the milk jug. Then he flew into the butter cask and then into the barrel of cornmeal. After that, the ugly duckling looked a sight!

The woman screamed and chased him with a broom. The children fell over each other trying to catch him. The ugly duckling barely managed to escape through the window!

The rest of that winter was lonely and difficult for the ugly duckling.

Then one day, he awoke to find the warm sun shining. Green leaves were budding on the trees. Beautiful spring had come at last! Joyfully, the ugly duckling spread his wings and flew. Soon he came to a pond.

Three proud swans were gliding across the water. When the ugly duckling saw them, he felt sadder than ever. "I will swim over to those beautiful, proud birds," he thought. "I am so ugly, they will surely kill me. But it will be better to be killed by them, than be bitten by ducks and pecked by hens and hated by everyone."

So he swam toward them with his head down to show he was prepared to die. It was then that the ugly duckling saw his reflection in the water. Instead of an ugly gray bird, he was snow-white with a long graceful neck. The ugly duckling had grown into a beautiful swan!

The three swans swam to him and stroked his neck with their beaks in welcome. Just then some children came running up to the edge of the pond. "Look!" they cried. "A new swan! Why, he is the most beautiful one of all!"

The once ugly duckling shyly ruffled his feathers and thought, "When I was the ugly duckling, I never dreamed I would ever be so happy!"